Tales
of BRAVE
and
Brilliant
GIRLS from the
GREEK
MYTHS

Tales of BRAVE and Brilliant GIRLS from the GREEK MYTHS

Retold by Susanna Davidson and Rosie Dickins

Illustrated by Josy Bloggs, Maribel Lechuga, Maxine Lee-Mackie and Wazza Pink

Contents

Foreword

The Ancient Greeks told each other stories to make sense of their world. Their myths brim with heroes and heroines, gods and goddesses, great battles waged, lives lost and loves won. Their stories have been retold for thousands of years but as they have been passed on, from one generation to the next, they have changed, both with the times and their teller.

For the last few hundred years, retellings of Greek myths have often had male characters at the heart of the story – from Zeus, king of the gods, to brave Perseus and wily Odysseus. The women have been left on the sidelines – often shown as passive, patiently waiting while the world moves on without them, or as dreaded monsters to be slain by heroes.

Now the stories are changing once again. Greek myths are beginning to be retold from the point of view of the women, just as they were in the writing of the Ancient Greek playwright, Euripedes, and the Roman poet, Ovid. And that is the aim of this book – to bring the female characters fully back to life and to make them the driving force of their own myths, in a way that is relevant to our own time. The girls and goddesses are not perfect. They are not always good. But they get to be the beating heart of their story.

You'll meet Gaia, goddess of the earth, born at the dawn of creation; Persephone, who ventures into the darkness, to make a new life for herself in the Underworld; and bold, brave Psyche, who risks her life for love.

There is Daphne, who must find a way to stay true to herself, and bewitching, magical Circe on her enchanted island. Listen to Penelope, as she tells her tale of cunning and survival, and discover Artemis, goddess of the wild, who sets out to outwit giants and rescue a god. There is fleet-footed Atalanta, who can outrun every man she meets and clever, dazzling Athena, who takes on one of the most powerful gods of all.

Read on to join them on their spirited, awe-inspiring adventures...

In Greek mythology, Gaia, born at the dawn
of time, was the great mother of all creation.

Gaia
- the first of them all

Every one of the Greek myths reaches back to Gaia. For the Ancient Greeks, she was both mother of creation and of the earth itself, worshipped as a giver of dreams and the nourisher of plants and young children. She came before all other gods, born at the dawn of time. Before her, there was nothing, and after her, came everything, for it was Gaia who brought it all into being.

Gaia

In the beginning, it was said, there was only blackness – no shapes, no space, no time, no borders. Just endless emptiness...

Then, one day, there was Gaia – the Earth goddess. She was warm. She was bold. She was beautiful. And she was brimming with ideas.

"What shall I create first?" she wondered, all alone in that vast void.

She thought of mountains and there they were, rising up from her fingertips, carved from jagged rock. She dreamed of waters and in swirled the sea, foaming and whirling, surging against her shores. Next came the rivers and the streams, weaving their way across the land, a beautiful branching pattern; then the sloping valleys and the green fields.

Gaia called the mountains Ourea, and the sea, Pontus, but she was not yet done. With Pontus she had five children, all gods and goddesses of the sea, full of wisdom and strength and wonder.

"Now I shall create something to lie between me and the darkness," Gaia decided, and she wove a being to arch above her in a vast dome. This was the sky, known as Ouranos, and it was love at first sight. When Gaia reached out to touch Ouranos for the first time, he blushed sunset red. By day, he bathed Gaia in light. By night, he lay like a coverlet over her, his darkness studded with stars.

Together they had twelve children – Titans, they called them – a race of giants, handsome and strong. Both Gaia and Ouranos looked at them proudly as they strode over the mountains and splashed in the seas.

And the Titans, in turn, had children of their own – gods and goddesses, who would divide the world between them. Poseidon took over the oceans and became their master, stirring the

foaming waters with his trident.
Zeus ruled the heavens with his
sister, Hera. Hades claimed the
Underworld, where gems lit the
gleaming cavern walls, and Hestia chose
to be goddess of the hearth and home.

That left only Demeter, who
looked down at her feet, placed on
the warm earth, among waving
grasses and bright flowers. Beneath
them she felt the tangle of roots, the
beginnings of new life. She placed her
hand on the bark of trees and listened to
them pulsing and whispering. She could
feel Gaia's energy running through her
fingertips, fizzing in her veins. And she
knew, then, that she wanted to help things
grow. She would coax grains from the bare
soil, care for every crop, help feed the
people who lived on the green earth.

She would be goddess of the harvest.

These gods and goddesses became known as the Olympians, ruling over ordinary men and women from their home, high up on Mount Olympus. It was the beginning of a new age and it was all begun by Gaia, the very first brave and brilliant girl of them all.

Demeter was goddess of the harvest.
Persephone, goddess of spring and
renewal, was her daughter.

Demeter and Persephone

Demeter was a green-fingered goddess. Her lightest touch or softest whisper was enough to make seeds sprout and fruit swell. She loved to watch new leaves unfurl, to make plants grow and grains ripen to gold. But by far her greatest love was her daughter, Persephone.

It was for Persephone that she grew the most beautiful flowers – delicate crocuses and tiny violets; enormous ruffled roses and long-stemmed lilies. Persephone would gather these in heavy bunches and bring them home, filling the air with their heady, sweet scents. Then they would sit, mother and daughter, talking and laughing late into the night.

Demeter was perfectly content with their life, and believed her daughter was equally happy. And Persephone *was* happy... on the surface. But beneath the surface, she was restless. She loved her mother, but she had begun to wonder what lay beyond the familiar woodlands and meadows that surrounded their home. She would gaze into the distance, longing to explore and meet new people, and daydream about the future.

One warm, golden afternoon, Persephone was out picking flowers. Birds chirruped and bees hummed busily as she plucked first a spray of white daisies, then a scarlet poppy. She paused to watch a bumble bee zigzagging to and fro, scattering tiny clouds of pollen. Then a huge butterfly fluttered past, towards a flower she had never seen before – dozens of tiny star-shaped blooms bursting from a single stem.

"How lovely," she thought, reaching out...

As she touched it, there was a low rumble. The ground shook, then split open before her, revealing a rocky path.

Persephone stared in astonishment. The path wound downwards, dark and mysterious and somehow inviting. Prickling with curiosity, she stepped forward. The path was cool and shadowed; the rock smooth under her feet.

As she walked on, the shadows deepened around her, until she was lost to view. Then, with a mighty *CRRRRACK*, the ground sprang together behind her.

No one saw her go, except Helios, god of the sun, who was shining brightly overhead. No one heard, except kind-hearted Hecate, goddess of magic, who was sitting by a cave weaving healing spells. Startled, she glanced up. In the distance, a handful of petals, scarlet and white, were still trembling on the grass. Hecate blinked thoughtfully and turned back to her work.

That evening, Demeter waited in vain for her daughter to come home. When Persephone did not return, she flung on a cloak and went out to look for her in the fading light. She walked the paths where Persephone liked to walk, and visited the meadows where she gathered flowers... but there was no sign of her.

"Where is my daughter?" Demeter demanded of the birds of the sky and the beasts of the earth.

They shook their heads mutely at her. None of them had an answer.

More desperately now, Demeter looked further afield, among the wild forests and across the distant hills... still, nothing.

As night fell, Demeter kept looking, stumbling heedlessly over dark roots and shadowy brambles, thinking only of finding her beloved daughter.

All night she searched until at last, in despair, she sought her friend, Hecate. It was not yet dawn, but she found Hecate already up and weaving her magic beneath a flickering torch.

Hecate told Demeter about that sudden sound. "I don't know what happened to Persephone," she said, "for I did not see — but there is one who sees all that happens by daylight." She pointed to a golden glow, just breaking over the horizon. "Come, we must hurry to catch him before he leaves."

The glow was Helios, the sun god. Each day, he set off at dawn, driving his fiery chariot from east to west across the heavens, bringing light and warmth to the world below.

The two goddesses found him about to depart, but he paused when he saw them. His team of horses stamped and tossed their heads, impatient to be off.

"Helios, lord of the sun, will you help us?" asked Hecate. "You look down and see all from your chariot in the sky."

"Did you see what happened to my daughter?" begged Demeter urgently. "Please, tell me."

Helios gave her a troubled look. He liked Demeter and knew how much she doted on her daughter. "Yes I saw her," he said. "She was picking flowers in the meadow when the earth itself split open and she walked inside. I believe it is

the doing of Hades."

"Hades!" exclaimed Demeter. Hades was a powerful god, brother of mighty Zeus himself.

"Yes," sighed Helios. "He has long admired your daughter, and hopes to make her Queen of the Underworld."

Just as Zeus, the king of the gods, ruled the skies and lands above ground, so Hades ruled everything that lay beneath. Known as the Underworld, it was the land of the dead – a dark, mysterious place deep below the earth.

Demeter imagined her daughter in that gloomy realm of shadows and spirits, and shivered. "I'm going to get her back," she declared.

"It won't be easy," warned Helios. "Hades is almost as powerful as Zeus."

Hecate raised an eyebrow. "Hades is not the only one with powers," she observed.

Demeter and Persephone

Demeter nodded stiffly. "Indeed, he has not reckoned with ME," she said.

"Good luck to you," said Helios, stepping into his golden chariot. "Now, I must be gone." He shook the reins and his horses sprang up eagerly into the sky, the light of dawn shimmering around them.

It was the dawn of a day like none the world had seen before. In her anger and grief, Demeter now stopped making things grow. Instead, she stormed and sighed and wept. Her sighs blew fierce gales across the land; her tears fell as icy rain.

Seeds stopped sprouting; shoots wilted, leaves drooped and turned black in the cold. Farmers watched in dismay as their crops withered in the fields. A bitter chill seeped into everything. People huddled miserably, trying to keep warm, as the very first winter settled over the world.

High on Mount Olympus, the home of the gods, Zeus felt the change and frowned.

"What is wrong?" he wondered. "And – *achoo!*

This dratted weather could make even a god catch a chill..." He peered down at the world below and his frown deepened. "The crops are failing. People will die if this continues."

Then he heard footsteps approaching. It was Demeter, Hecate still at her side.

"There will be no harvest," she said in a low voice. "No fruit on the trees, no grain in the fields. Nothing will grow on earth until my daughter returns to me."

Zeus looked into Demeter's pale, set face and nodded. Her determination was clear. He might have been king of the gods, but he did not want to come between a mother and her child – especially a mother as powerful as Demeter. He snapped his fingers.

"Hermes, come here!"

The messenger god flew up at once. The feathery wings on his golden sandals fluttered as he bowed respectfully.

"Hermes, go and tell Hades he must bring Persephone back to her mother immediately."

With a flick of his feathered heels, Hermes obeyed.

He didn't take long to reach the Underworld.

Hades lounged on a high throne of smooth black stone. Persephone sat comfortably on an identical throne beside him. A huge, three-headed dog lay at her feet, gazing up at her devotedly, while all around them thronged a court of whispering ghosts.

Hermes had thought to find Persephone sad and homesick, but her eyes were dry and she greeted her visitor with a contented smile. Hermes even thought she looked... happy?

In spite of Demeter's fears, Persephone had been enjoying herself. It had been an adventure, exploring the Underworld.

And Hades had done his very best to charm her. He had met her in the darkness, and apologized for not approaching her in the ordinary way. "I have spent so long down here, I hardly know how to appear above ground," he had admitted.

Then, he had shown her wonders: vast underground fields of scented lilies; glittering crystal caverns; sparkling piles of gold and heaps of jewels

Then, he had shown her wonders: vast underground fields of scented lilies; glittering crystal caverns...

mined from the belly of the earth. He had promised
her mysteries and the undying adoration of the
spirits who inhabited his realm. "All the treasures of
my kingdom are yours," he had told her, with dark,
pleading eyes. "If you will have them?"

For Helios had been right; Hades wanted
Persephone to become a queen and rule the
Underworld at his side.

Persephone had found she enjoyed talking
to Hades and delighted in spending time with
him. She had been intrigued by his dark realm, so
different from her mother's home. She had been
so busy exploring, she had hardly missed the sunlit
meadows of the world above...

Now, Hermes' pleas brought it all back to her.
"In her grief, your mother will not let anything
grow and the world is suffering badly," he said
urgently. "Zeus himself commands you to return!"

Persephone and Hades exchanged a look.
Hermes, watching carefully, sensed something
pass between them. He had thought Hades would

protest – but instead the god nodded in agreement.

"Indeed, you should go back to your mother," Hades said to Persephone. "But before you go, tell me – have you been happy here?"

"Yes," said Persephone readily.

"Have you been well treated, and gone where you pleased?"

"Yes," she said again.

"And have you eaten?"

"No." Persephone shook her head.

"May I offer you something before you go?" Hades held out a silver dish, on which the sweet red seeds of a pomegranate gleamed like rubies in the gloom.

"Wait!" gasped Hermes, trying to snatch the dish away. But it was too late. Persephone, with decisive fingers, had taken a pinch of seeds and swallowed them.

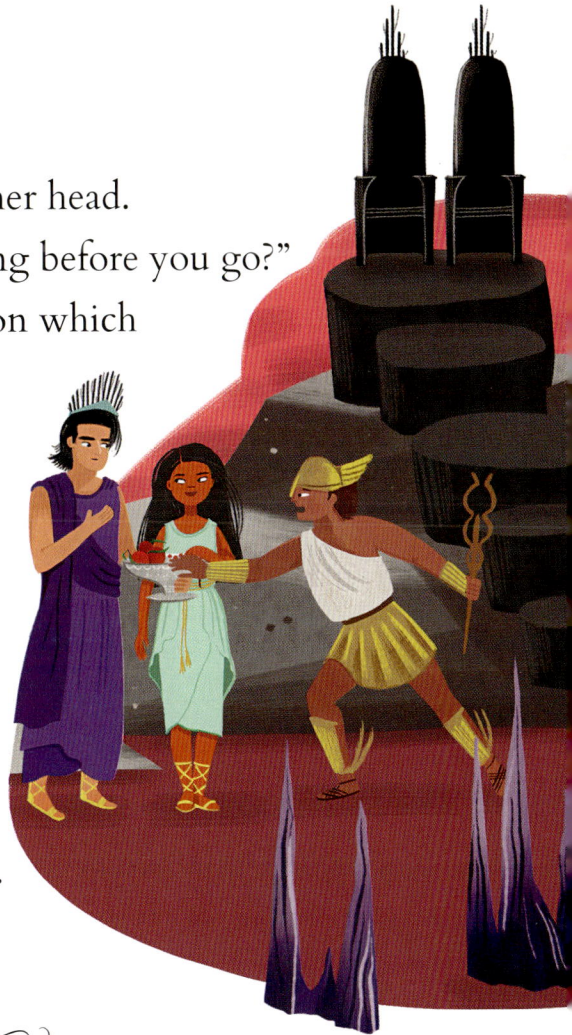

Hades beamed with relief. "As we all know, the ancient law dictates that anyone who eats in the Underworld must remain here. Persephone, my dear, it seems you will be staying after all."

Persephone smiled back at him – but there was something in her expression that Hades, for all his powers, could not fathom. Not for the first time, he wished he knew what she was really thinking.

Hermes was indignant: "The order for her to return came from Zeus himself!"

Zeus was the king of the gods; an order from him could not just be ignored.

"Then this will have to be settled by Zeus," observed Persephone calmly. "Come – let us go and see him."

"I'm coming too," added Hades quickly – afraid that if he didn't, Demeter would somehow stop Persephone from returning.

"Oh, very well," snapped Hermes.

So when Hermes returned to Mount Olympus, he brought not one but TWO others with him.

"Persephone!" cried Demeter, running to embrace her daughter with happy tears.

Persephone threw her arms around her mother, hugging her tight. But then she pulled away, turned and took the hand of the god behind her.

"Hades!" snapped Demeter, her voice like icicles. "What are YOU doing here?"

"I have come to make my case."

"What case?"

"Oh, Mother, don't be angry..." pleaded Persephone. "But I ate six pomegranate seeds in the Underworld."

Hades gave a triumphant grin. "You know the law..." he began.

Demeter turned pale and turned to Zeus. "Only six seeds! Six tiny specks... that cannot be enough to make her stay down there."

"But she ate them, so stay she must!" said Hades.

"If she stays in the Underworld, I shall never make anything grow again!" stormed Demeter.

"Enough," interrupted Zeus, in a voice that

rumbled like thunder. Everyone fell silent.
Zeus gave Persephone a long, searching look.
Persephone met his eyes with a direct stare of her
own. She wondered if HE could read her thoughts;
if he would understand why she had eaten, but
eaten so little...

Zeus nodded thoughtfully. "Did you eat those
seeds of your own free will?" he asked.

"Yes," said Persephone.

Zeus smiled at her. "Then I rule thus: for six
seeds, you shall spend six months of each year in the
Underworld with Hades. The rest of the year, you
shall spend with your mother on earth."

Demeter and Hades glowered at each other, but
Zeus had spoken. His word was law.

Persephone beamed. "Thank you," she told Zeus
sincerely. He had understood perfectly. Now, she
would not have to choose between one place or the
other, but could divide her time equally.

So for half the year, Persephone would live as
Queen of the Underworld, ruling over the land

of darkness with Hades. And for half the year, she would enjoy the sunlit meadows with her mother.

While Persephone was away, Demeter let the leaves fall and winter storms blow. But when it was time for her to return, Demeter welcomed her back with sunny smiles and carpets of spring flowers.

So Persephone was daughter *and* Queen, living between two worlds and making both her own.

Psyche was born a princess and went
on to become goddess of the soul.

The Tasks of Psyche

Princess Psyche supposed she was lucky. She was a princess, after all, and she knew she was greatly admired for her beauty. Poets wrote songs praising the depth of her eyes and the waves of her hair. Artists begged for the chance to capture her likeness in paint or stone. But, sometimes, beauty can be a burden...

Psyche's looks made her sisters jealous and strangers nervous. Some would stammer and blush in her presence. Others whispered behind their hands and avoided looking her in the eye. So, although she had many admirers, Psyche had no close friends.

"Oh, how I wish I had someone to talk to," she would sigh.

Worse still, people gossiped about her. A beauty like hers, they said, did not belong to mere mortals. "She must be related to the gods," they claimed. "Truly, she's more lovely than Aphrodite herself!"

Up on Mount Olympus, Aphrodite, goddess of love, heard the scandalous comments. "More lovely than ME?" she fumed. "I can't have people saying that. Hmm, let's see..."

She thought for a moment, then smiled coolly and called out for her son. "Eros!"

In an instant, a curly-haired youth stood before her, a quiver of arrows slung over one shoulder. They were magical arrows, a gift from his mother.

Anyone hit by one would fall instantly, hopelessly in love.

"Eros, I want you to find a mortal named Psyche and make her fall in love with someone AWFUL. A truly hideous monster! She'll become a laughing stock..."

Eros bowed. "As you wish, Mother," he promised and flew off to do her bidding.

He found Psyche wandering over a hill near her palace. But as he gazed upon her, his heart melted as if pierced by one of his own arrows. "What has this girl done to deserve my mother's punishment?" he thought. "She can't help her looks! I won't harm her. But my mother might... I should get her to safety!"

As he considered the matter, a light breeze ruffled his hair. "Zephyrus?" he called, recognizing the touch of his old friend, the west wind.

A playful gust answered him.

"Zephyrus, I need you to carry this girl to my castle in secret."

Far below, Psyche felt a strong gust of wind lift her into the air. "Wh-what's happening?"

It was strange but, at the same time, so gentle that she did not feel afraid. Another gust and she was flying over the landscape. Tiny houses and trees and fields sped by below. Psyche laughed in delight and exhilaration.

The wind set her down in front of a high castle of smooth, white stone.

"Hello?" she called. There was no answer, but the castle's enormous door swung open, almost inviting her inside. Psyche stepped through, into a grand entrance hall lined with golden columns and sparkling gemstones.

"Is anyone there?" she tried. Again, there was no reply, but another door opened. "I should explore," she decided. "Then perhaps I'll find some clues to what's going on..."

Psyche walked
through room
after room, all
as magnificent
as the first
golden hall.
Each held a
new luxury. There
were tables heaped with dainty
foods... couches of silken cushions...
piles of interesting books and
exquisite musical instruments... but
not a single other soul.

"Well, I might as well make myself
comfortable," she decided. So she settled down
amongst the silken cushions and started to read.
When it grew dark, golden lamps flickered into life.
When she grew tired, she settled back against the
couch and the lights dimmed. She had almost fallen
asleep when... RAT-A-TAT!

There was a knock at the door.

"Who's there?" she called, suddenly wide awake, her heart pounding.

"I can't tell you my name," came the reply. It sounded like a young man's voice. A friendly young man. "I just wanted to make sure you're all right. Do you like the castle?"

"It's lovely!" exclaimed Psyche. "And I have everything I need. Well, except someone to talk to – but I'm used to that."

"Um... well, would you like to talk to *me*?" offered the voice, a little shyly.

"Why not?" thought Psyche. "Yes," she replied. And then, remembering her manners, "Yes please. Do come in."

At that, the door opened and someone entered. The room was so dark, Psyche couldn't see his face. She reached for a lamp.

"No!" said the visitor at once, his voice suddenly urgent. "You cannot see me."

Psyche frowned, but chose not to argue. So many strange things had happened already, what was one more oddity?

She and the mysterious visitor talked for hours. From palace life and politics to poetry and painting, they discussed EVERYTHING. He seemed to enjoy their talk as much as she did, for he returned again the next night, and the next... For the first time in her life, Psyche felt she had found a real friend.

Just one thing puzzled her. Why wouldn't her new friend reveal his name or let her see his face? "He's hiding something," she reasoned. "But what?"

Back at home, her sisters had liked to tease her by saying she would spend her life with a monster. "There's a prophecy," they would tell her smugly. Psyche had thought they were making it up, but now she wasn't so sure. "What if he IS a monster and this is a trap?" she wondered. "I've got to find out!"

The next night, she and the visitor talked until they both felt drowsy. Yawning, he got up to leave as usual.

"Please, don't go," said Psyche. "It's late. Why not stay and sleep here?"

"All right," he agreed, settling back into his couch. "Thank you."

Psyche waited until she heard gentle snores. Slowly, silently, she tiptoed over to a lamp and lit it. She held it up high, so its light fell on the slumbering figure... and gasped.

This was no monster. Soft curls framed the most handsome face she had ever seen. Psyche recognized a god when she saw one. "Eros!"

As she spoke, a drop of hot oil fell from the lamp and splashed onto Eros, waking him. His eyes widened as he met Psyche's gaze. Then a spell broke and the castle vanished – taking Eros with it. Psyche found herself standing alone in a dark forest.

"Oh Eros, I'm sorry!" she cried. "Where have you gone?" She thought of their friendship and uttered a desperate prayer. "Aphrodite, goddess of love, hear my plea. Eros is your son. How can I find him again?"

Aphrodite heard the prayer with a smile, delighted to have the princess at her mercy. She appeared with dazzling radiance, making Psyche blink. "You won't EVER see my son again, unless you prove yourself worthy," she told the princess coldly.

Psyche looked the goddess boldly in the eye. "How?" she asked.

"I will set you three tasks. If you complete them all, I will bring you to Eros. Fail, and you will be parted forever."

Psyche lifted her chin. "I am ready."

"Very well. You can start by sorting these!" Aphrodite snapped her fingers and a muddled mountain of grains poured onto the ground out of nowhere: barley, oats, wheat, millet... "You have until daybreak!" And, with that, the goddess vanished.

There was no time to waste. Psyche kneeled down on the cold, stony ground, scooped up a handful and set to work. Straining to see in the inky dark, she picked at the grains, placing each type in a separate heap. When the whole handful was sorted, she took another. She worked until her eyes smarted and her fingers ached – but the mountain hardly seemed to grow any smaller. Something tickled her toes. She glanced down and saw an army of ants marching around her feet. She thought they had come to eat the grain and was about to brush them away when she realized... "Oh! You're helping. Thank you." By the time the first rays of sun broke the horizon, every grain was sorted. Moments later, Aphrodite reappeared.

The goddess gazed at the neatly sorted piles and frowned. She had hoped Psyche would fail. "Never mind," she thought to herself. "There are still two more tasks." She raised an arm, bracelets jangling, and pointed to a distant meadow. "Look!"

Psyche looked. The meadow was dotted with grazing sheep.

"Bring me some of their wool."

Psyche set off. As she neared the meadow, a soft wind rustled the grass and she heard a warning sigh: "The sheep are dangerous! Do not go near them."

"Thank you," she whispered. Now she was closer, she could see they were no ordinary sheep. They had fierce eyes and sharp horns, and their fleecy coats flickered with a golden fire. How could she gather their wool without approaching them?

Psyche glanced around, thinking. Here and there, brambles and thorns poked above the long meadow grass. Tiny tufts of golden wool fluttered on some of them, where sheep had snagged their coats while grazing. "That's it!"

Careful to avoid the sheep, she darted from thornbush to thornbush, until she had a large, soft handful. She carried it back to Aphrodite, who took it with pursed lips. "Let's see how this girl deals with REAL danger," the goddess decided.

"Follow me!" Aphrodite led Psyche to a rocky cavern. It was too deep and shadowy to see what lay inside, but the sound of trickling water echoed from somewhere. "Bring me some water from that spring. Hurry now!"

Psyche picked her way cautiously through the gloom. As she approached the water, something huge and scaly slithered out of the rocks ahead. She caught a flash of wicked teeth and claws.

"A dragon!" she realized, heart pounding. "It must be guarding the spring. How can I get past it?"

A harsh cry made her look up. A golden eagle was swooping down. As she watched, it skimmed the water and sent up a spray of sparkling droplets. Quickly, Psyche stretched out her arms and caught a glittering handful.

Quickly, Psyche stretched out her arms
and caught a glittering handful.

Carefully, so as not to spill a drop, she climbed back to Aphrodite. "Here is your water. I have completed your tasks. Where is Eros?"

But Aphrodite wasn't about to stop. She was ready with a fourth task. "To find Eros, you must now visit the Underworld."

Psyche was brave, but even she paled at that. *The land of the dead?* Ringed by a river of darkness, it was guarded by Cerberus, a fierce, three-headed dog. Charon, the boatman, ferried dead souls across the river, but the living never ventured there.

"Persephone, Queen of the Underworld, has an enchanted box," continued Aphrodite. "Bring it to me, and I will bring you to Eros."

Psyche set off with a heavy heart. "To reach the land of the dead, I suppose I must die," she told herself, and sighed sadly.

Then she felt a soft breeze brush her cheek and heard a whisper... "No! There is another way. Find the entrance and you can cross into the Underworld alive. Make sure to take a honey cake for Cerberus and two coins for Charon. Once you are across the river, speak to no one but the Queen."

Psyche took a cake and coins, and followed the wind's whispered directions until she reached a remote cave. The mouth of the cave was narrow and forbidding. Swallowing hard, she squeezed through and went on.

Rocky walls dripped and stones crunched underfoot. Ahead of her, something stirred. Three noses sniffed the air, three pairs of glowing eyes turned in her direction and three ominous growls made the air tremble.

"Good dog," she said, with more confidence than she felt. "I've brought you a treat." Quickly, she broke the honey cake into three pieces... snuffle, gobble, gulp... and Cerberus wagged his tail like a puppy.

The Tasks of Psyche

Psyche went on, down the passageway he had been guarding. Now the ground sloped ever more steeply down, until it reached an underground river. The black water flowed sluggishly, like molten glass, completely blocking the way.

Psyche held out a coin and Charon, the boatman, appeared. He ferried her across in silence.

On the far side, ghostly figures drifted about, murmuring faintly. Psyche swallowed her fear and tried not to look at them as she walked up to Queen Persephone and curtseyed. Persephone smiled mysteriously and held out a small, carved box.

"Thank you," whispered Psyche. The box felt strangely heavy as she carried it back to the

river. Another coin for the boatman, three pats for the three-headed dog – and she emerged into the sunlight with a rush of relief that it had all been so straightforward. She didn't know the danger she was carrying...

Psyche weighed the box in her hand. "I wonder what's making it so heavy?" Curious, she lifted the lid. At once, the enchantment of the Underworld washed over her. She swayed briefly, then fell to the ground, as pale and still as death.

As Psyche went about her tasks, Eros had been secretly watching over her. He was powerless to stop his mother, but he had done his best to help Psyche – the whispers in the wind had come from him.

But when Psyche completed three tasks, only to be set a fourth, he realized: "My mother will never stop, and I can't make her... but I know someone who can!"

So while Psyche was in the Underworld, he flew off to find Zeus, king of the gods, and told him the whole story. "Please, help us!"

Zeus was touched by Psyche's devotion. "This girl has proved herself brave and loyal. She deserves to join the gods. I will make her an Immortal, so she can be with you forever."

Beaming, Eros flew back to Psyche... only to find her lifeless. She lay like death beside the open box, whose misty tendrils still wound their way around her.

"Oh, no! The enchantment!" Quickly, Eros drew the magic away, replacing it in the box and closing the lid.

He watched his friend anxiously, waiting...

For a long moment, nothing happened. Then,

very slowly, Psyche's eyes fluttered open. The first thing she saw was Eros' dazzling smile. Now at last he could tell her everything, from Aphrodite's jealousy to Zeus' promise of immortality.

"So we can be together always," he finished happily. "No more hiding in the dark!"

"Friends forever," agreed Psyche, smiling back. "Just what I've always wanted."

Daphne was a water nymph,
the daughter of a river god. Her
name means 'laurel' in Greek.

Daphne's Transformation

Daphne had always felt she wasn't like the other girls. All her friends loved to go into town, to meet and to mingle, trying on new robes, tasting the food sold at the market, making new friends...

"Join us," they would call to her, as they strolled past, laughing and smiling.

As always, Daphne would wave to them and smile back, but shake her head. She preferred to stay where she was, here by the river.

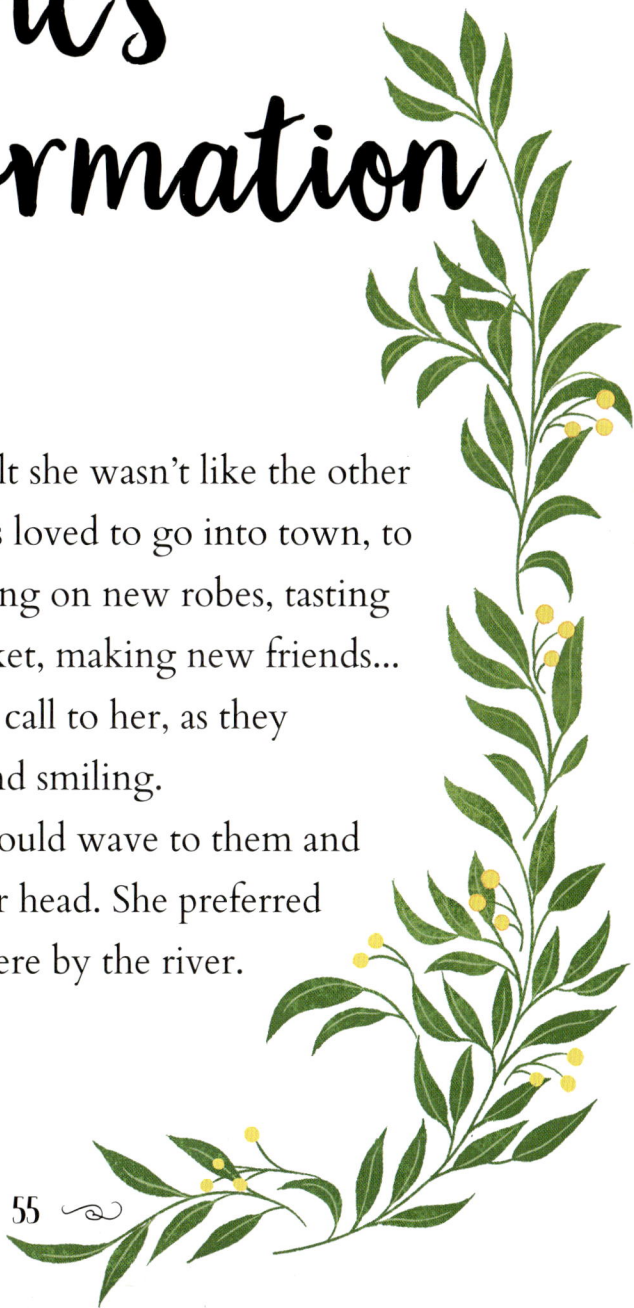

Daphne's Transformation

Perhaps, she thought, it was because she was a water nymph... Her father, Peneus, was a river god, after all, so no wonder she was at her happiest by the river, where the waters ran cool and clear. She would tangle her fingers in the tall rushes, dip her toes in the swirling foam and close her eyes in blissful contentment.

Daphne loved to go into the mountains, too, with her pack of hounds and her bow and arrow. But even then, when out hunting, she was never far from water – the gurgle of mountain streams singing in her ears as she strung her bow and aimed her arrows, straight and true. She would listen

to the wind, which seemed to speak to her as it whispered over the hills or rustled in the groves.

"If only," she sighed, "my life could always be this way."

"Nonsense," said her father. "What about falling in love? Don't you want to get married one day?"

Daphne shook her head and her father laughed.

"You'll change your mind," he said. "And what about me? Don't I deserve a son-in-law? And grandchildren, to call my own?"

Daphne hugged him then, but still she shook her head. "Can't we agree that I'll never marry?" she said. "Zeus granted the goddess Artemis that wish. Can't that be true for me too?"

Her father sighed. "If that is what you really want," he said.

"It is," Daphne swore.

And she stayed true to her word.

Many men fell in love with her, but Daphne said no to them all. They did not quicken her heart. She felt that it beat only for the rushing wind, the flowing river and the mountain streams.

She watched her friends marry, one by one, but she never changed her mind, however much they teased her.

Instead, she loved to gather the other nymphs around her. Together, they would swim in the water and run through the long grasses that lined the banks. *But to marry... no. That,* Daphne told herself, *will never happen.*

"You may not be a goddess," said her father, "but in your own way, you are as brave as one. You've forged your own path."

But Peneus wasn't the only god who knew of Daphne's dreams. Far away, on lofty Mount Olympus, Eros, god of love, had learned of them too. He had watched and listened, full of mischief, his bright eyes twinkling. "So Daphne never wants to marry?" he mused. "A beautiful girl who spurns men. That could come in useful one day..."

The day came sooner than he thought, for Apollo, god of archery, dance and poetry; god of music, healing and the sun, was currently swaggering around Mount Olympus, puffed full of pride. He had just killed Python, a huge serpent, and was giddy with his own success. He saw Eros, peering through the clouds, and laughed at him.

"Look at you, god of love, with your bow and arrows," he mocked. "What could you possibly do with them? Nothing compared to me! I fire my arrows and wound wild beasts! I slay my enemies! And now I've fired my arrows at Python, that great swollen serpent, whose coils weighed down the land, spreading disease. And what happened then? Why, I killed him, of course! Could you ever do anything like that? Ha! *Never!* All you do is make people fall in love!"

Eros sat and listened, and hid his fury well. "You may defeat all with your arrows, Apollo," he thought, "but I shall overcome you!"

When Apollo had gone, Eros looked down once more at the world beneath the clouds. There was Daphne, still wandering happily in the woodland groves. "Yes, you will do very nicely," he decided. "It will be the perfect revenge for that puffed up Apollo. I'll make him fall in love with you, and you'll never fall for him. Then Apollo will feel the power of love and discover what it's like to be mocked."

On those words, Eros put a golden arrow to his bow and fired it straight into Apollo's heart. Apollo didn't feel a thing. The gold struck home and melted, spreading its potion of love until it coursed through Apollo's veins, ringing out Daphne's name.

"And just to be sure..." murmured Eros, putting

another arrow to his bow. This one was blunted and made of lead. He aimed it straight at Daphne and, when it struck her heart, it deadened every last ounce of love she may have felt for men.

Soon after, befuddled with love, Apollo made his way to the woodland grove where Daphne lay resting. No sooner had he looked at her than she had his heart. He was lit up with love, aglow like the setting sun.

But Daphne took one look at him and ran – through the forest, slipping between the trees that whispered to her, their branches brushing her sides, as if helping her on her way.

"Wait!" called Apollo. "Come back! I just want to talk to you..."

But Daphne wouldn't wait. She had known at

once that this was a god, from his golden glow, his luminous beauty, his arrogant stride. She wouldn't stand a chance if he caught her.

"I don't want to talk," she called back, as she ran. "I just want to be left alone."

"But I need you," said Apollo, following behind, swift as a deer, his hair glinting in the sunlight.

"No," insisted Daphne, her determination giving her courage.

They ran through the forest, up hills and down again, along the gurgling streams. Daphne was swift. She was a hunter, after all, who had spent her life outdoors. She knew every corner of the forest, every rock, every boulder, every dip and curve of

Daphne's Transformation

the green hills. She ran like the wind, but she was no match for a god.

At first, Apollo held back. He didn't want to scare her. But, proud as he was, he was sure that soon Daphne would turn and really look at him, and then she would love him, just as he loved her.

"Slow down," he begged. "Stop awhile. Don't scratch yourself on these thorns. Don't tear your feet on the jagged rocks."

Daphne ran on.

"Your hair flows like the river," Apollo sang. "Your skin gleams like the sun."

His compliments fell on stony ground. Daphne left them for the crows to pick at, and ran on.

"You are more beautiful to me than everything in this green valley," Apollo went on.

"Just go," said Daphne. "Please, GO!"

"Your eyes shine like stars!" shouted Apollo.

Daphne's breath was coming in ragged pants now. She needed to find help.

She called out to her father, the river god. "Can you make Apollo stop? He won't listen to me. Tell him I am not the one for him. Say I have sworn never to marry."

But her father was no match for Apollo.

"I don't have that power," he replied, his voice carried on the burbling streams. "Apollo is god of poetry, music and archery. He may be worthy of your love?"

Would Daphne have wavered? Perhaps... perhaps not... but with Eros' leaden poison locked in her heart, she was far beyond persuasion.

"Who can help me now?" Daphne wondered. And in that moment, she knew. She needed someone who could match Apollo for power; she needed Gaia, goddess of the earth.

"Gaia!" Daphne pleaded. "What can you do?"

The earth rumbled in reply. Boulders shook. The air was thick with thunder. "I cannot stop Apollo," came Gaia's voice. "But I can take you back – deep into the earth, where you'll be safe."

Daphne turned around. Apollo wasn't far behind. "Would I ever get out again?" she asked.

"No," said Gaia, sadly. "You would become part of the soil."

"So I'd never see the sky again," said Daphne. "I'd never feel the wind against my skin, or hear the song of the river, or see the turn of the seasons..."

"Never," said Gaia. Then she took a breath. "There is one more thing I could do for you..."

Even as she spoke, Apollo had come closer still. Daphne had run, fast as a hare, and he had come after her, full of hope, and now he was almost there.

"I could change you," said Gaia, "into something living, but not human – a blade of grass, a flower, a tree..."

"Into a tree," gasped Daphne. "Change me now!"

"Are you sure?" asked Gaia.

Daphne's Transformation

Her arms raised, twisted, turned to branches;
her whole body encased in a trunk.

"I'm sure," said Daphne, bravely, determined. "This is what I want..."

Just as Apollo reached Daphne, her skin became thin, smooth bark. Her arms raised, twisted, turned to branches; her whole body encased in a trunk. Her hair fell as rustling leaves, silvered in the sunlit breeze.

Apollo stopped and stared. There was no girl to love there, just a laurel tree.

"Oh Daphne," he called, his voice full of regret and sorrow. "We could have been so happy, you and I." But, even then, he didn't stop to think what he had done to her.

And what of Daphne? Could she still think? Could she still feel?

She could. Beneath her thin skin of bark, deep in her trunk, in the heartwood, Daphne smiled. She was safe at last. She was rooted to the earth, but still she would grow.

She reached down and felt her roots pulsing through the soil. She could taste the moisture there, the minerals, all the earthy richness of the world below the sun.

She reached up and felt her branch-arms tangling in the breeze, the wonder of the sun on her green leaves. Beside her lay the river, ever-changing, and the valley, with its long grasses tickling her trunk.

She sighed with contentment. "Thank you," she said to Gaia. "This will suit me very well."

Apollo reached out to touch her smooth, slender trunk, but then drew back, sensing at last that he had not been wanted.

"I could have given you all my love," he said. "Immortality, even."

"Immortality?" thought Daphne. "I will still have a long life. In time, my trunk will crack and knot with age. I will grow thicker, stronger. I am here to stay. I'll never have to fight to be alone again."

Apollo was on his knees now, Eros' golden potion still burning through him like a flame. "Even though I am the god of healing... despite knowing

the power of every herb that grows, I cannot cure this love or heal this pain."

He stepped away from the tree. It was shining with beauty. "Perhaps I may wear a wreath of your leaves as a crown?" he asked. "I would wear it with respect."

Daphne waved her branches, to show her consent. "And may that crown be a reminder," she thought, "of what happened here."

Gently, Apollo tugged off some sprigs of leaves and wove them around his head. And then he left.

Daphne let out a long sigh. She let her branches dance in the wind. She murmured to the song of the river. She plunged her roots deeper into the soft earth. "And now," she thought, "goodbye to the girl. Time to let my tree-life begin."

Circe was goddess of sorcery. She
was the daughter of Helios, the sun
god, and the ocean nymph, Perse.

Circe the Sorceress

Circe had always known there were goddesses far more powerful than her. She could reel off their names and titles. "Athena, goddess of war. Aphrodite, goddess of love. Hera, goddess of marriage and queen of them all..."

She would see them, occasionally, when visiting their home on Mount Olympus. She would watch them, peering down through the clouds to spy on mortals, laughing and playing with their little lives.

Circe was nothing like those goddesses – and whenever she came across them, they were happy to remind her of that fact.

"Your father may be the sun god, but your mother was only a nymph," they would say. "You don't belong on Mount Olympus with us, in our palace among the clouds."

Instead, Circe spent her days on a small island, Aeaea, tending to flowers and herbs, picking fruit from her trees, busy in her garden or at her loom.

"I don't need a gleaming palace among the clouds," Circe told herself. "I don't want the company of gods and goddesses. I have something far better, something that is with me always... my knowledge of potions and herbs."

The others called her a witch, and Circe basked in that word. Her magic was a source of both power and pride.

She had been born with it, coursing and fizzing and crackling though her veins. But it was only through hard work that she had mastered it. Circe had performed her magic, over and over, just as she worked at her loom or her garden. And she needed the power it gave her – to make her strong, to protect her and, she had to admit, to have a little fun, now and again...

All the herbs and flowers on her island were for her potions. Each morning, she picked them, shredding and stirring and boiling, making and re-making her brews until each was perfect for its allotted task.

As for the words of her spells – they came to her in her dreams and she chanted them in song. Over time, her mind had become a library of spells she could call up at will.

Her first potions had been to tame the lions and wolves on Aeaea, so they wandered the island as gentle as lambs, and slept like dogs at the foot of her bed.

Next, she began
on the art of
transformation,
changing worms
to birds, and
birds to bears,
and back again.
She made herself
a magic staff from the
branch of a yew tree and,
when she needed to, she placed enchantments on
those who passed her way.

Often, Circe used her magic wisely and well, to
help, to protect and to heal. But sometimes, when
her emotions grew too strong, when she felt lonely
or hurt, she had the irresistible urge to use her
magic for more selfish ends.

When a king named Picus rejected her, Circe
chanted a spell in anger – and turned him into a
woodpecker. Worse still, perhaps, was the revenge
she took on the sea nymph, Scylla. Mean-spirited,

scornful Scylla... She had always looked down on
Circe and when Glaucos, the sea god, fell in love
with Scylla – *how* she had boasted about it! Scylla told
Circe that Glaucos *worshipped* her. She recounted
all the adoring things he'd whispered to her, even
though she knew she was breaking Circe's heart;
for Circe had fallen in love with Glaucos herself.

The night Scylla had taunted her, Circe had
gone to bed furious, to wake with a spell on her lips
and a potion brewing and bubbling in her mind.
She picked her herbs at dawn, when they were at
their most potent. In went poisonous juices and
sprinklings of night, deadly crushed berries and
leaves rotten with blight. She chopped and ground
and stirred until the mixture was ready. Then she
put on her cloak and sailed to a narrow strip of sea,
where she knew Scylla loved to bathe.

Circe poured the potion into the water, leaving
inky, wraith-like trails. Moments later, Scylla,
beautiful Scylla, slipped into the water, her hair
swirling around her like silk. Circe watched from

behind a rock as Scylla began to scream. The potion
was working its wicked magic. First, Scylla's neck
split six ways. Gone was her beautiful face, replaced
by six grisly heads full of jagged, dagger-like teeth.
Her body became twelve writhing tentacles; her
waist ringed by snarling dogs' heads.

Screaming still, Scylla scrabbled up the
rocks that loomed next to the sea. She
clung there, open-mouthed, already
greedy for food. Her eyes were
beadily fixed on the waves,
looking for sailors on
whom to feast.

Circe watched it all, transfixed. She felt a curious mixture of horror at what she had done, and delight at her own power.

"Although maybe," she thought, gazing at those snapping jaws and blood-shot eyes, "I've gone a *little* too far this time."

From then on, word had spread about her skill. Now she was known not as a minor goddess on an obscure island, but as a great and powerful witch.

And so, when twenty-two sailors washed up on Circe's shores one day, she didn't hesitate to act.

"I have my brilliant reputation to maintain, after all," she thought.

She offered the sailors barley, cheese and golden honey, and goblets of dark, red wine. Then she slipped into their food a special potion, brewed from jimson weed. As they wolfed down their food, guzzling and gobbling, Circe touched them with her staff... and the men began to change.

First, thick hog-bristles sprouted out over their skin. Two pointed ears rose up from their scalps.

Two legs became four and then, yes... there were twenty-one pigs, snorting and grunting around her table.

Their noses lengthened, ending in wet, snuffling snouts. Two legs become four and then, yes… there were twenty-one pigs, snorting and grunting around her table.

"How odd," she thought, counting them again. "What has become of the other man?" Still, Circe was sure one man alone could not be a threat to her, so she herded the others into a pen behind her house and fed them, generously, she thought, on pig nuts.

Hours later, came a knock at the door. "Was this the twenty-second man?" she wondered. Circe led him to a silver-studded chair and offered him a drink, mixed with the same potion as before. But when she went to touch him with her staff, to transform him as she had all the others, nothing happened. Instead, the man knocked the staff from her hand.

"What have you done to my men?" he hissed.

"Who are you?" Circe retorted. She stood tall, refusing to back away. "No mortal can drink my potion and not be bewitched."

Her mind raced. The only way to escape her
enchantment was with the help of the moly plant –
with its black root and milk-white flower. But only
a god could pull a moly plant from the ground…

"Who helped you?" she demanded.

"The god, Hermes," the man admitted. "One of
my men raced back to the ship and told me what
you had done to the others. As I made my way
here, Hermes came to me and offered me a plant I
had never seen before. He said the only way to save
myself, and my men, was to eat it before I met you."

"Ah," said Circe. "Then you must be Odysseus,
come at last."

Hermes, the winged messenger, had told her
about Odysseus long ago… how this man would
come to her island on his swift ship and that he
would not be bewitched by her magic; that his wits
would be a match for her own.

Odysseus nodded. "That is my name," he said.
But he didn't take his eyes from hers. "Now, you
must swear a god's oath that you will not harm me."

"I swear it," sighed Circe.

"And that you will free my men."

"I'll free them," Circe replied, turning away from him. "Although I do think you could teach them better manners."

Odysseus and his men stayed on Circe's island for a year. They were worn down and broken-hearted from months at sea, their minds like the morning fog, their eyes blank. But, day by day, Circe saw to it that their energy was restored. She gave them clean tunics to wear. They feasted at her table and drank her sweet wine. They rested on her golden sands and bathed in her perfumed oils. And every night, Odysseus would tell Circe of his travels – how he was sailing back from a war, desperate to reach Ithaca, his island home.

He could tell a good story, Odysseus, with his deep, honeyed voice, as thick and sweet as Circe's wine. When he talked, she listened, spellbound, to the tales he span. *Were they all true?* she wondered, his stories of the Land of the Lotus Eaters, his battles with the one-eyed cyclopes and the man-eating giants... She thought, perhaps, Odysseus was as much of a magician as she was, weaving his magic with words. By the time a year had passed, she was in love with him, even though she knew he longed to go.

"My men are desperate for home," Odysseus told her. "We are rested now. We must set sail again."

Circe wished with all her heart that Odysseus would stay, but still, she helped him on his way.

"First," she said, "you must go to the

Underworld, where Hades rules, and ask the prophet Tiresias for advice. The North Wind's breath will blow you there. Tiresias will tell you about your journey and how you may reach home again. It will not be easy."

Then she told him of other dangers he would face: the sea monster, Charybdis, who loved to suck sailors down to their watery graves; of Scylla, watching from the rocks, ready to lunge with her six long necks and snatch up sailors in her gruesome, toothsome jaws.

She sent food and supplies down to his ship, and watched as Odysseus and his men set off across the sea once more.

"Now I am alone again," she thought. "Alone with my garden and my loom and my potions. Still, he was only a mortal man," she told herself. "His life will slip away while mine runs on."

But with each passing month after Odysseus left, Circe's body grew fuller, her belly rounder, and by the ninth month she had given birth to a son.

Circe named him Telegonus. As a baby, he would play with her mountain lions and sharp-clawed wolves, snuggling up by their side. As her smiling, brown-eyed boy, Telegonus loved to watch Circe at work on her spells. And she loved him back, for filling the island with his laughter, for keeping her company while all the world went by.

But by the time Telegonus was full-grown, he would sit on the island's rocks and gaze out to sea, asking question after question. *What lies beyond the horizon? What is life like, beyond this small island? Who is my father?*

Circe knew he deserved answers. She told him all about Odysseus, and Ithaca, the island he came from. And when Telegonus begged to leave and find his father, Circe helped her son set sail, just as she had helped Odysseus, all those years before. But fearing for his safety, she gave him a poisoned spear, spiked with the spine of a stingray.

Months passed. Circe found herself on the dark rocks, scanning the horizon, longing to see her

son's ship come home, wondering how he fared. *How would Odysseus greet him? Would Telegonus face danger along the way?*

And then at last, one morning, just as the rosy-fingered dawn lit the sky, she saw his white sails fluttering in the breeze, and his ship came ashore on the golden sands.

Circe ran down to the beach to greet him. "Telegonus, my son, you're home at last," she cried.

But his shoulders were slumped, his head bent, and with him were two strangers – a man and a woman.

Circe the Sorceress

"I killed him, Mother," said Telegonus, tears in his eyes. "I arrived in Ithaca, carried there by a storm. I was so hungry, my men and I began plundering the city, searching for food. Two men rushed out... I tried to explain who I was and what I was doing, but they wouldn't listen. I fought with the older man. I used the poisoned spear to defend myself... and I killed him. Only then did I realize who it was – Odysseus – my own father."

Circe went to comfort her son. "And what happened then?" she asked gently.

"I was told it was Odysseus' wish to be buried here, so I have brought his body back to Aeaea.

And I have brought his wife, Penelope, and his other son, Telemachus, too."

And he introduced the strangers.

"Come," said Circe, holding out her hands to them. "You must be hungry. Let me feed you – on barley, cheese and golden honey, and goblets of dark, red wine."

Circe the Sorceress

Circe had made a decision. There was a debt to be paid here. And so she prepared a potion, slipping it into the food. But this one was not laced with the poisonous jimson weed. This potion was different.

As Penelope and her son, Telemachus, ate at her table, Circe touched them with her staff and whispered her spell.

This time, she was giving them a gift she too possessed – that of immortality. As she touched them, she saw their bodies begin to glimmer and glow, to shine that god-like light.

They didn't understand, yet, of course, what she had done. She would tell them in time. But first, she drew Penelope to one side and asked, "What is your story? I am sure that you, too, have a tale to tell..."

Penelope was daughter of Icarius, one of the kings
of Sparta, and the water nymph, Periboea.
She went on to become Queen of Ithaca.

Penelope's Tale

I was born a princess, and I was born clever, so you could say I had an easy start in life. My father was a king of Sparta and my mother was a naiad – a water nymph.

My childhood, in our beautiful palace, was golden. But as soon as I was of marrying age, my father arranged a contest, a running race, as was our custom. I was to marry the fastest man – and that man was Odysseus, ruler of the Kingdom of Ithaca.

Later, when I knew him better, I wondered if Odysseus had won the race by trickery. I had soon discovered that he was as a cunning man, with a mind to match my own. I also heard that Odysseus had done a deal with my uncle: he'd helped to arrange the marriage of my cousin, Helen, in return for me. So perhaps my uncle had helped Odysseus win the race. Do I mind if that story is true? No, of course not. One of the reasons I came to love Odysseus was for the clever workings of his brain.

Once I was married, my father expected us to stay in Sparta, but Odysseus wanted us to return to his kingdom. As Odysseus and I drove away in his chariot, my father chased after us, begging me to stay. I lowered my veil and looked my father in the eye. I didn't say a word. I just looked at him, and then at my husband, and at once my father understood. I had chosen to go with my husband, even if it was improper to say so out loud. After that, my father let me go, to begin my new life...

At first, everything was like a dream — a perfect

dream. Odysseus' parents welcomed me into the family. His old nurse, Eurycleia, fussed over me. And Ithaca itself was beautiful. An island lying low in the water, far, far out to sea. A land of sunsets and gently sloping hills, olive groves and wild oaks, winding paths and tumbled stones. I felt at home there from the very first.

In our palace, Odysseus carved a bed with his own hands, from a living olive tree whose roots sank deep beneath the palace floor. "Like our loyalty to each other, this bed can never be moved," he said.

My joy was sealed with the birth of our baby boy, Telemachus. We doted on him, a happy gurgling baby with a smile as warm as the sun. But it wasn't long after his birth that the quiet rumblings began...

...rumblings that would one day shatter our world.

First came the news that Paris, the Prince of Troy, had run off with my cousin, Helen. Her husband, King Menelaus, was determined to get her back. Helen's beauty was known throughout the world, so much so that, before she married, all her suitors had to swear a solemn oath to defend her chosen husband. And Odysseus had been one of those suitors.

He shook his head at the news. "There'll be a war," he said. "I know it. All of us will have to go with Menelaus to Troy, to bring Helen back. Who knows how long that will last... And who knows how long it will take me to get home again."

"It could be a quick war," I said.

But Odysseus looked at me bleakly and then away at the rolling sea. "An oracle told me once that if I went to war with Troy, my journey home would be longer than I could imagine."

"Then we can't let you go," I replied, full of the confidence of youth. "Together, we'll find a way."

We stayed up all night, plotting, and by morning, as Menelaus' ship came into view on that sunlit sea, Odysseus left the house, ready to carry out our plan.

"I'm here for Odysseus," Menelaus announced when he arrived, full of his usual swagger, his friend Palamedes at his side.

"Odysseus isn't well," I told them, wringing my hands. "You can take him to war with you, but he'll be no use."

"What do you mean?" demanded Menelaus.

I could see Palamedes, looking at me through narrowed eyes. Palamedes, I knew, would be harder to fool than Menelaus.

"It's his mind," I whispered, as if afraid to put the truth into words. "He... he... Go and see for yourselves. He's out in the fields."

They went to look, puzzled frowns on their faces. And there was Odysseus, driving a donkey and an ox, sowing our fields with salt.

"What is he *doing*?" demanded Menelaus. "Has he lost his mind?"

I could only nod and brush the brimming tears from my eyes.

Menelaus went up to Odysseus and tried to talk to him, to reason with him, but Odysseus simply stared straight ahead, as if his mind was wandering in another world.

"I've had enough of this," muttered Palamedes and he turned to go inside.

Perhaps he's leaving? I thought, hopefully. But when he returned, he had our baby, Telemachus, in his arms.

"What are you doing?" I cried, running after him. "Give me back my baby!"

But Palamedes refused to break his stride. He laid Telemachus down in the field, directly in front of the beasts.

"If he's truly crazy," said Palamedes, a grim smile playing about his lips, "he'll run over his own son, won't he? And if he's not, he'll swerve."

I could only watch, distraught, as the donkey and ox came ever closer to our baby. I tried to go to him, but Palamedes held me back. I knew Odysseus would never harm our son, but still, I could hardly bear to watch...

At the last moment, Odysseus swerved. Of course he swerved – what father wouldn't? Palamedes gave a shout of triumph and our fate was sealed. That very day, Odysseus went to war.

And how long was he gone? How long did the war last? One year? Perhaps two? Let me tell you... the war lasted ten long years. I raised our son, alone. I looked after the fields, the palace, the kingdom, the servants. Odysseus' mother died and his father, Laertes, became an old man. Stories of Odysseus' truimphs in war came back to us. *And how did I feel?* Proud, fearful and frustrated too – all those years we should have had together, swallowed up by the war in Troy and that fight between Menelaus and Paris and my oh-so-beautiful cousin, Helen. Athena, the powerful goddess of war, was on Odysseus' side, they said, so I hoped for his swift return. But it did not come.

After the war, other soldiers came back to their homes, but not mine. *Oh, no!* That would have been too easy. Instead, news would reach me of Odysseus' trials at sea. Somehow, he had angered Poseidon, god of the sea, and now Poseidon was doing all he could to stop Odysseus from coming home.

At first I clung to the stories I heard. I fed on them. They told me that Odysseus was still alive. That he was *trying* to come home. But, in time, the stories that reached us became more ragged, more threadbare, woven out of imagination, thin on facts, until at last, there was no fresh news at all. Everyone thought Odysseus must be dead. And that's when my troubles *really* began.

The men of Ithaca began to swarm into my house, first as a trickle and then as a flood. They ate my

food. They drank my wine. They lived off my land and wasted its wealth. But of course I knew what they were there for... they all thought Odysseus was dead and they wanted to marry *me*. My son called them *the suitors* and hated them. I did too. They paid me compliments from dawn to dusk, but any fool could see they were longing to step into Odysseus' shoes and have Ithaca for themselves. I was Queen of Ithaca and each one wanted to be King.

I could stop all my troubles in a moment and marry one of them. But I had hope in my heart... what if Odyssesus was still alive?

I had no one to help me. Odysseus' father was too old. My son was too young. On my side, I had Eurycleia, Odysseus' nurse (ancient as the hills) and a few loyal servants.

I turned to my father, asking for his help, but he only told me to come back to Sparta and marry again. *Never*, I thought to myself. My cousin, Helen, may have been celebrated as the most beautiful woman alive, but I was as clever as she was fair. So, after years of suffering the suitors' attentions, I concocted a plan of my own. I told the suitors that I would choose one of them for my husband, but only once I had finished weaving a shroud for Odysseus' father, in preparation for the day he died. That seemed to keep them quiet.

And then, my weaving began. By day, I stood at my loom, working away. At night, by lamplight, I unpicked what I had done. It sounds easy. It was not. Do you weave? If you do, you will know that for every strip of fabric I had made, I had to pass the shuttle over and under the threads again, in the same pattern as the day before, but in *reverse*.

By day, I stood at my loom, working away. At night, by lamplight, I unpicked what I had done. It sounds easy. It was not.

It was exacting. It was exhausting. No wonder I cried all the time. This went on for *three years*. But for those three years, my plan worked. The suitors were kept at bay.

In my heart, I'd hoped that Odysseus would return before the shroud was done, but still there was no sign of him.

Next, came the betrayal. One of my own maids told the suitors what I was up to and they declared they would wait for me no more. I had to choose one of them for my husband. With each passing day, they became more persistent. I was fast running out of hope.

Then, one morning, I discovered that my son, Telemachus, had gone. He had set sail to find news of his father. Worse still, I was told, the suitors were plotting to kill him when he returned. I prayed to the goddess, Athena, and that night I dreamt that Telamachus would come home safely.

"And what of Odysseus?" I asked in my prayers. But there was no answer.

The next day, I berated the suitors. I called them brutish. Sneaks! Criminals! "How could you plot to kill my son?" I cried. "This has to stop!"

Of course they placated me. They told me they were plotting no such thing. I did not believe them. All I could do was trust in Athena, and that trust was well placed.

Telamachus did return, unharmed. I flung my arms around him and showered his face with kisses, my own face wet with tears.

"Is there any news of your father?" I asked.

And what he told me gave me hope again – that Odysseus had been trapped on an island by the nymph, Calypso. And then a man, who had returned with Telemachus, spoke too. He told me that Odysseus had escaped the nymph and was already in Ithaca, plotting his revenge against the suitors.

❧ Penelope's Tale ❧

How I longed to believe him. But I did not dare, not yet...

Later that night, news reached me of a beggar, come to our palace, who said he knew Odysseus. My heart beat fast at the news. I asked for the beggar to come to me, so I could question him about my husband. And when at last he came, I invited him to sit on a cushioned chair by the fire. There he told me that Odysseus was still alive, and would soon be home.

Penelope's Tale

The beggar told me his name was Aethon and
that he was from Crete. But the more he spoke, the
more familiar he seemed, until at last, I knew him
for who he was. This was *my* Odysseus. He was in
disguise, but I would know him anywhere.

Why did he not reveal himself to me? I wondered.
He must have had his reasons. So I stayed quiet,
even though my heart was melting. I played along
with his tricks. I told the servants to make him up a
bed with fresh clean sheets and to bathe and oil him.

And then I thought up a plan of my own.

Once my husband had washed, I came to him.
"I will set up a contest for the suitors," I said, still
pretending I thought him a beggar. "I will arrange
for Odysseus' axes to be set in a row, and I will
marry the man who can shoot an arrow through all
twelve axes, just as Odysseus could do."

And my husband, not guessing that I knew who
he was, readily agreed to my plan.

The next day, I asked Telemachus to set up the
axes. One by one, the suitors tried the task, and one

by one, they failed. I was not there to see it, but it was told to me. Only Odysseus, of course, could do it. He strung his bow and shot the arrow clean through the line of axes.

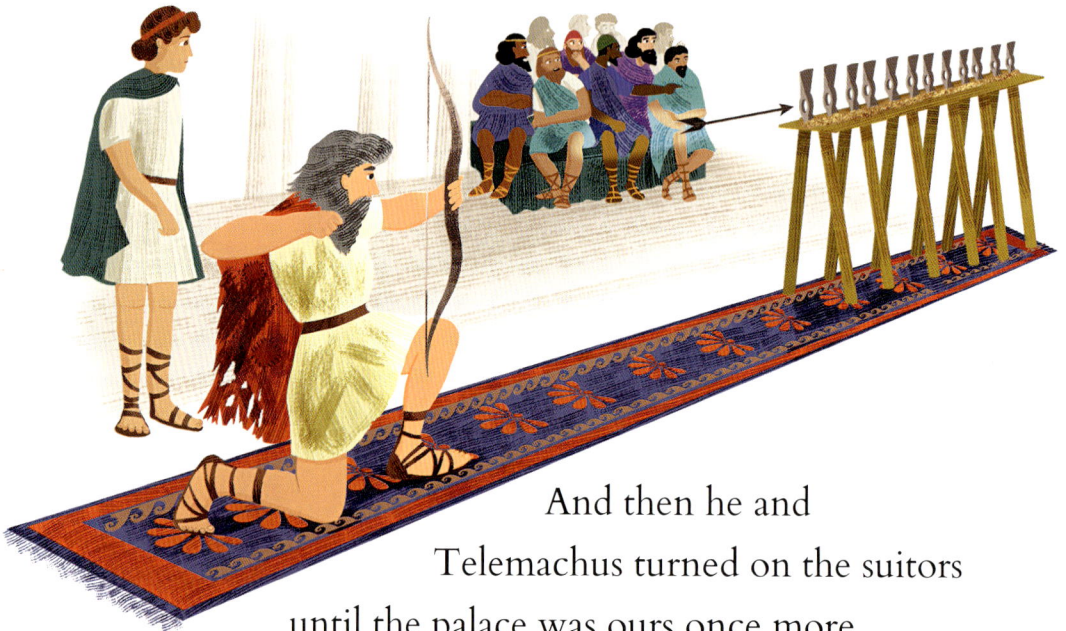

And then he and Telemachus turned on the suitors until the palace was ours once more. When I was brought the news, I came downstairs. Odysseus stood before me now, undisguised. But twenty years had passed since we last saw each other. How different he looked, and how different must I have seemed to him. He stood beside a pillar, keeping his eyes down. I wanted to go to him, but I stood there, stunned.

"What are you doing, Mother?" demanded Telemachus. "Why don't you go to your husband, my father? Is your heart made of stone?"

But Odysseus only smiled. "Twenty years is a long while to be apart," he said. "Give us time."

Odysseus went away. He washed. He bathed. He came back dressed in a tunic and a rich cloak. Again, he sat down opposite me.

Then he turned to Eurycleia, his old nurse. "Make a bed for me, so I can rest," he asked.

But even though I knew him, I wanted to test him. Still I couldn't fully trust that Odysseus had really come back to me. What if the gods were up to their tricks again?

"Eurycleia," I said. "Make up a bed for him outside our room. Pull out our old bed and cover it with quilts and blankets."

Odysseus – and now I knew it really must be him – looked furious. "You cannot move our bed! What have you done to it? I carved it from the olive tree that grows in our courtyard. The bedposts are made from the trunk itself."

And now I knew, beyond doubt, this was my husband, come home at last. I ran to him then, and we held each other and wept together.

That night, Odysseus told me of his travels and I told him of what had happened while he had been away. *Did we tell each other everything*? I think not. Too much time had passed.

Not everyone would think this a love story. We had been twenty years apart. But still, it's a fairy tale to me. We both survived with our wits. We both made our way back to each other.

When the poets retell our story, I know Odysseus will be celebrated as a hero. They will sing songs about him. Just as he wove magic with

his words, so will the storytellers – recounting how he fought at Troy, helped bring back Helen, and had many adventures at sea. But there are two sides to every story, and I think mine has its own, quieter heroism. For twenty years I protected Ithaca. I raised our son. I tricked the men who tried to steal the kingdom from Odysseus. I'm glad to have the chance to tell my story. For it, too, deserves to be heard.

Artemis, daughter of Zeus, was goddess
of wild animals, the moon and hunting.
She was also a protector of girls.

Artemis
and the Hunt

If you went looking for Artemis, you'd find her in the mountains. Or maybe running in the forests after fast-trotting deer. Or if not there, then skimming, light-footed, over the marshes, where the earth turns to muddy pools and the croaking of frogs fills the air.

But wherever you found her, it would be outside, even on the darkest of nights, for Artemis was goddess of the wild.

Artemis and the Hunt

She was so much a part of nature that she could turn herself into an animal at will – a deer, a wild boar, a hawk – and do the same to others. But even though she was a protector of animals, she was a fierce hunter of them too...

If you saw Artemis, you would know her by her golden bow. When she felt like it, she would stand on a mountain top and shower the wind with her arrows, which flashed down like deadly rain. And she loved to hunt: she loved the chase, knowing the thrill of her skill, but she knew when to stop, too. And when she had hunted her fill, she would put down her bow and arrows, and rest in shady groves, or dance with the tree nymphs to bubbling, beating music that thrummed like the hum of the earth itself.

Artemis and the Hunt

Artemis was known to the other gods and goddesses as both brave and bold. As a small child, she had sat with her father, Zeus, and told him all her wishes.

"I wish never to be married," she said. "To have a bow and arrows; and always wear a hunting tunic. To bring light to the world..."

"Anything else?" Zeus had asked, laughing.

Artemis nodded, deeply serious. "I would like sixty nymphs for my friends, to help me care for my dogs, and to have all the mountains as my domain."

While others had gasped at her audacity, Zeus, king of the gods, had been unable to resist. He had granted his little daughter each and every one of her wishes. He had a golden bow and arrows made for her by the Cyclopes, the one eyed-giants who had forged Zeus his own powerful thunderbolt.

Artemis went herself to collect them, all the way to the tiny isle of Lipara. Next, she visited Pan, god of the forest, who gave her thirteen hounds to hunt with. And then she spent her growing years

perfecting her hunting skills, until each arrow she
drew hit its mark, unfailingly, no matter how swift
or cunning her prey. In time, she rewarded herself
by catching a pair of stags, to pull her
golden chariot through the wilds.

So it was no surprise that
when there was hunting to
be done, the gods turned to
Artemis. And on this particular
day, it was Hermes who was
sent to find her. The winged
messenger god skimmed
the clouds, looking down at the forests and
the marshes and the fields, until at last he saw
her, in a quiet grove beside a river.

"It's the Aloadae," Hermes said, breathlessly, when he reached Artemis' side. "They're making trouble again."

"The giants?" said Artemis, casting her mind back. She remembered talk of them from years ago – two brothers, Doom and Nightmare, sons of Poseidon, the god of the sea. Even at the age of nine they had stood taller than the loftiest trees. Artemis remembered them as aggressive and highly skilled; not to be crossed, even back then.

"They haven't stopped growing," Hermes went on. "Each day they grow ever taller and stronger, and now even Zeus himself is afraid of them. They have stolen Ares, god of war, and bound him in chains on the Island of Naxos. No one can free him. He's has been trapped there for twelve months and if one more moon waxes and wanes... I'm afraid he will be no more."

"Then I will go to him," said Artemis, reaching for her bow and arrows even as she spoke. "I will set him free."

"Wait!" said Hermes. "There is more. The Aloadae are boasting that next they will storm the heavens – the home of the gods themselves. They say they will move mountains to reach us, piling them on top of each other, and when they get there, they will claim two goddesses as their wives."

"Who?" asked Artemis, going very still.

"Hera, queen of the gods... and you."

Artemis glowered. "How dare they! They cannot claim us against our will. Besides, don't they know I have sworn never to marry?"

Hermes could only shrug. "I don't think they care much for that. It is Doom who wants you for his wife. Nightmare has chosen Hera. They need to be stopped."

"Don't worry – that's exactly what I plan to do."

"There's just one problem," said Hermes, holding up his hand as he saw Artemis getting ready to leave. "These giants are so strong now, and so powerful, Zeus thinks that no god can stop them."

Artemis sank back down again.

"Really?" she said. "Unstoppable, even to Zeus?"
Hermes nodded.

Artemis took a deep breath, her fists clenched.
"I will find a way," she vowed.

That night, while the moon shone bright and
her nymphs danced through the woodland, Artemis
plotted and planned. If all the gods combined
couldn't defeat the Aloadae, then what chance did
she stand? It seemed impossible. But to lose... and to
have to marry one? That was unthinkable.

The giants would be too strong for her arrows,
Artemis reasoned. What other skills did she possess?
She could turn into an animal of the woods, but
how would that help her? She
could never outrun them.
There was no pit deep
enough to bury them.
No river wide enough
to stop them...
Her mind
whirling, Artemis

called for her stags and hitched them to her golden chariot. She would ride through the night, she decided, and see if a plan came to her.

Off she sped, through the tangled woods and forests, up and down the stormy mountains, until she reached the windswept marshes, all silvered in the moonlight. And there, among the croaking frogs, were the night herons, silently stalking. Artemis watched as one darted forward and snapped a frog in its long, spike-like beak. Then out of the shadows came another heron and set upon the first, trying to snatch the frog. One heron, fighting the other. "That's it!" said Artemis, as she watched. "Set one giant against the other... *That's* how I'll do it!"

By morning, Artemis was close to the Aloadae. They hadn't been hard to track, their vast footprints leaving great marks in the ground all the way to Naxos. And they had left a trail of devastation in their wake. Trees were uprooted, hills flattened, riverbanks downtrodden and destroyed.

She heard them before she saw them. Their

footsteps rumbled the ground like earthquakes. Their shouts reverberated in the still morning air. She could hear them, easily, discussing their plans to storm the home of the gods. Their bodies cast shadows as long as mountains over the day and when she saw them, she gasped. Their legs were wider and taller than the highest trees. Their bodies blotted out the sun, their heads reaching up almost to the heavens.

Now was the time, Artemis knew. She set her thoughts to the deer of the forests... their sleek pointed hooves, their bright brown fur and pricked ears. When she looked down at herself again, she had transformed into a deer.

Her black nose twitched. Her tail quivered. Then, with a shake of her slender head, she ran on, bounding between the giants, leaping from boulder to boulder, scattering stones as she went.

The Aloadae looked down. They saw the deer darting between them.

"Let's catch it!" cried Doom, eager as ever to

"Now!" cried Doom and Nightmare together. Then they raised their tree-like spears and hurled them into the air.

hunt and to kill. And he raised his giant spear.

"I think I have it," cried Nightmare, raising his spear too.

Artemis ran on, careful to weave between them, edging first closer to one and then to the other, but moving too swiftly for their huge spears.

Full of frustration, the brothers shook their fists and growled. They furiously kicked at massive boulders and gouged rocks from the earth, sending them tumbling through the sky.

Ahead, Artemis saw a hill and began to climb, her breath coming in fast pants, the thundering footsteps of the Aloadae close behind.

She waited until they were on either side of her and then she stopped, bowing her head as if exhausted, her flanks heaving.

"Now!" cried Doom and Nightmare together. Then they raised their tree-like spears and hurled them into the air.

In a flash, Artemis dived forwards. The spears crossed in the air. Doom's spear pierced Nightmare, gliding deep into his heart. Nightmare's spear struck Doom in the same place, just as deep.

The Aloadae looked at each other, their faces full of horror as Artemis took back her goddess form. Too late, they realized they had been tricked. Down they fell to their deaths, their angry cries rending the air; then silence. Peaceful silence.

Artemis hurried on to Naxos, and freed Ares from his chains. Then she returned with him, triumphant, to Mount Olympus, home of the gods.

And there, in their palace above the clouds, the gods celebrated.

Zeus smiled at his daughter. "Stay a while and feast with us."

But Artemis shook

her head. She called for her stags and her golden chariot and waved goodbye to the other gods.

"If you need me, you know where to find me," she said. "In the mountains or the forest or the marshes, or wandering through the night."

And if you see Artemis, you will know her by her golden bow and arrows. Unless, of course, she has transformed herself. For she could also be that fleeting deer you passed in the forest, ears pricked, tail aquiver.

Atalanta was a child of the
wilderness, and much-loved
by the goddess Artemis.

Atalanta's Race

Atalanta grew up in the wilderness, with wolves and bears as playmates. She had been abandoned as a baby, swaddled in a blanket and left on a rocky mountainside – but Artemis, goddess of the wild, had watched over her and kept her from harm.

It was Artemis who had sent a great brown she-bear lumbering up to the bundle. The bear snuffled curiously at the blanket with a large furry nose. The blanket squirmed and chuckled, and a dimpled hand reached up to touch the tickly fur...

"*A cub?*" the bear thought. "A human cub, but still – a cub. And a cub needs a mother." So the bear gently picked up Atalanta in her mouth and carried her to her den, to care for alongside her own cubs.

As a cub, Atalanta learned the ways of the wild animals, and the mountains and forests where they lived. It was a rough and tumble life, and Atalanta loved it. Like the bears, she was fierce and strong and free-spirited. As soon as she could walk, she roamed widely and without fear, perfectly at home in the wilds.

One day, Atalanta was exploring in the forest when she smelled something unfamiliar. She sniffed curiously... it was rich and spicy, and it made her tummy rumble. Following her nose, she came to a clearing. In the middle, a pile of wood was spitting and smoking, while a little boy watched an old huntsman poke a pot above it. When the boy saw Atalanta peeking out, he gave a cheerful wave. The old huntsman looked up and smiled, and held out a hunk of bread. Atalanta hesitated, then took it. A bowlful of steaming stew followed, and a new friendship was born.

The old huntsman saw the wildness in Atalanta's eyes, but he also saw a little girl in need of a home and a human family to look after her.

"Would you like to meet the rest of our family?" he asked. Atalanta looked at him, uncomprehending. So he held out a hand and Atalanta, curious, took it. He led her through the forest, to a cluster of wooden huts. Kind faces appeared in the doorways to greet them.

There, Atalanta learned the language and the
ways of people – although she did not forget
her old life altogether. Sometimes she would run
off and disappear for days on end, exploring or
foraging with the animals, coming back with torn,
berry-stained clothes and tangled hair. There was
no stopping her. She could outrun the huntsman
and everyone else in his village.

When she was older, the huntsman taught her
to use a bow and arrow. She quickly became a fine
shot. Her hand never trembled. But her greatest
skill was running. She could run faster than anyone,
human or animal. She loved to race over the
mountains, until the world was a blur
and her lungs gasped for air,
for the sheer joy of speed.

Perhaps a little of the wilderness stayed in
Atalanta's heart, because she eventually left the
village to live in the mountains again. On those
steep slopes, she felt free. She didn't dream about
finding a sweetheart and getting married, like the
village girls. She wanted to live alone among the
animals, like the goddess Artemis – a goddess she
greatly admired.

Her home was a mossy cave, tucked away
behind a clump of pines. Twining ivy grew around
the entrance. A gurgling stream gave her water.
The forest kept her well fed with berries, nuts and
roots. She thought she would go unnoticed. But
she was wrong...

Hunters glimpsed her running between the
trees. A farmer spotted her climbing rocks.
A goatherd saw her standing on a high peak, hair
blowing in the wind. They admired her careless
grace, her strength and speed – and they told others
about her. Soon after that, men began appearing in
the mountains.

The first time, Atalanta returned to her cave to find a young man waiting nervously outside. When he saw her, he dropped to his knees and begged her to marry him.

Atalanta was not impressed. "I don't want to get married," she said stubbornly. "That's why I came to live up here on my own. Now go away and leave me in peace!"

But a few days later, there was a second young man, also asking for her hand in marriage. And he was followed by another and another... Atalanta always gave the same answer, but more and more young men kept coming.

Sometimes, one of them would try to woo her with a long, flowery speech, but Atalanta had little patience with such talk. As soon as he began, she would cut him short by saying: "Oh very well, I will marry you if you can run faster than me."

Then they would race and Atalanta would win, as she had known she would, and the young man would turn away, defeated.

Once she had beaten her suitors, Atalanta didn't give them a second thought. She didn't care about any man's feelings – until she met Melanion.

Melanion was a young hunter with unruly hair, who loved the wilds as much as Atalanta. He had seen her in the forest, and couldn't stop thinking about her. Now he came to her cave and asked if she would race against him, as she had raced so many others.

"You hope to win my hand in marriage?" Atalanta sighed.

"I hope to win a little time with you," said Melanion shyly. "That is all."

"So you don't want to marry me?" Atalanta was intrigued.

"I might," Melanion confessed, his face turning pink. "But not

because of some race. You're a person, not a prize!
I'd just like to get to know you..." He gave her an
earnest, hopeful look.

Atalanta met his eyes and felt a pang. She
wouldn't enjoy beating this young man.

"Don't challenge me," she warned. "You'll never
win. I grew up running with the wolves and bears."

"I'll take my chance," insisted Melanion.

Eventually, against her better judgment,
Atalanta agreed to a race the next day.

Melanion was bold, but he wasn't foolish. He
was a good runner, but Atalanta was the best. If he
was going to stand a chance, he would need help.

"Aphrodite, goddess of love, please help me,"
he prayed that night. He wasn't sure what to
expect, perhaps a sign or omen of some kind...

Instead, to his astonishment, the room filled
with a soft, pearly glow. The light flickered for a
moment and then he was looking at a beautiful
woman with shining hair. It was Aphrodite herself,
and she was holding out three golden apples.

"Take these," she told Melanion.
"They come from the tree of the gods."

"Th-thank you," stuttered Melanion.

Aphrodite dropped the apples into his outstretched hands.

Thunk, thunk, thunk! They felt smooth and warm, and surprisingly heavy. The gold glimmered enticingly as he gazed down at them.

Aphrodite smiled. "Lovely, aren't they? And I guarantee Atalanta will think so too. Use them to distract her, and you may win your race."

A faint breath of wind stirred. Melanion glanced up. The room was back in darkness. The goddess was gone. He blinked, then looked back at the apples in his hands.

"Is this cheating?" he wondered. "But I can't ignore a gift from a goddess... and I DO want to impress Atalanta. What should I do?" He drew a long breath, considering. "I'll take the apples with me," he decided at last. "But I won't use them unless I really need them."

When Melanion arrived for the race, the hunter's bag he always carried was bulging and chinking oddly. A small crowd had already gathered around Atalanta's cave to watch.

Atalanta gave him a rueful smile. "I can't persuade you to change your mind?"

Melanion shook his head firmly. "No. I want this too much."

"Very well," she sighed. "We'll race to the old oak tree way over there. Are you ready? Three, two, one... Go!"

And so the race began... At first, Melanion and Atalanta were neck and neck. Their feet flashed and trees passed in a blur. Melanion ran faster than he had ever run before. But Atalanta was faster still.

Slowly but surely, Atalanta drew ahead...

Thunk! A golden apple dropped heavily to the ground. Atalanta looked around, puzzled. Melanion, feet pounding desperately, saw her hesitate – then dart back to scoop it up. As she did so, Melanion raced past her.

Atalanta sprang to her feet and began running again. In a few strides, she had caught up with Melanion. Then she passed him. He tried to match her speed, but she was too fast...

Thunk! Another apple.

Again, Atalanta paused, then ran over to pick it up. Melanion was back in the lead. But not for long. In two strides, Atalanta closed the gap. For a moment the runners were side by side, then she was out in front. Melanion could see the gap lengthening.

THUNK! In desperation, he threw the last apple as hard as he could. Atalanta glanced at it, torn. She knew if she stopped again, she would lose the race.

The gold gleamed in the sunshine...
and Atalanta ran to the golden apple.

But she wasn't sure how much she wanted to win. The gold gleamed in the sunshine... and Atalanta ran to the golden apple.

As her fingers closed around the golden orb, the crowd erupted in cheers. Melanion had reached the oak tree. The race was over and he had won. He leaned on the tree for a moment to catch his breath, then turned to see Atalanta's reaction.

To his relief, she didn't look upset.

"Congratulations," she said calmly. "You dropped something," she added, holding up three golden apples.

Melanion ducked his head guiltily. "Yes," he admitted. "I was trying to distract you. Sorry, I know that wasn't very sporting. The apples were a gift from Aphrodite, when I prayed to her for help. My excuse is that I *really* wanted to win – and I knew I wouldn't have a chance otherwise..."

"All this, just to spend time with me?" asked Atalanta, intrigued.

Melanion nodded.

"Very well then," she replied. "Let's start..."
Melanion beamed.

Atalanta and Melanion spent the rest of the day walking and talking and laughing in each other's company. Each thought they had never been happier. The next day, they did the same... and the next, and the next... until it was clear to everyone, they were perfectly suited to each other.

Atalanta had only one worry – she didn't want to leave her beloved mountains.

"I am so happy here," she prayed to Artemis. "Please let Melanion understand."

Melanion, for his part, was so wrapped up in Atalanta that he didn't make any prayers at all. He didn't even offer thanks to Aphrodite for her help.

Both goddesses were watching the young couple. Artemis had heard Atalanta's prayers, and was wondering how best to answer her. Aphrodite simply wanted to see what happened. As the goddess of love, she was delighted that she had helped to bring this pair together.

But, as the days passed and Melanion gave not so much as a whisper of thanks, her delight changed first to impatience and then to anger. It is always unwise to forget your manners, but never more so than when dealing with a goddess.

Aphrodite did not like being taken for granted. "That boy owes his happiness to me," she hissed.

"And see how he repays me! I'll teach him a lesson. I'll turn the pair of them into... into..."

Aphrodite was a powerful goddess. She could turn them into anything she chose. Artemis thought fast. "Lions?" she suggested, a hint of a smile dancing in her eyes.

"YES!" cried Aphrodite. She snapped her fingers... Below in the forest, Melanion and Atalanta suddenly fell onto all fours.

"Wh-wh-what?" they gasped in astonishment, as their skin sprouted velvety golden fur and their shape melted and changed... Whiskers sprang up beside their noses, claws curved out from their fingers and toes. When they tried to speak again, it came out as a rumbling yowl.

In the place of the two young humans, there now stood two powerful lions. Their long, tufted tails whisked the grass as they looked around, senses sharp and muscles strong.

Then Atalanta gave a roar of satisfaction and raced off, thrilled with her new, four-footed swiftness. Melanion shook out his gleaming mane and bounded happily after her.

"Prayer granted," Artemis thought, with relief. It might not have been quite what Atalanta had imagined, but now she could live happily in the mountains with Melanion for the rest of her days.

Athena, also known as Pallas Athena, was goddess of wisdom, weaving and warfare.

Athena's Gift

All gods are extraordinary, but the bright-eyed goddess Athena was more extraordinary than most – and from the very beginning. They say she was not born, and was never a child, but leaped fully-grown out of the head of great Zeus himself. It was a strange start, even for the gods, who are used to marvels.

On the day Athena sprang into being, Zeus, the king of the gods, had woken up with a terrible headache. His groans rumbled like thunder around the heavens, as he screwed up his eyes and clutched his forehead.

"HEPHAESTUS!" he bellowed desperately. His son, the god of blacksmiths, came running.

"My head is SPLITTING," moaned Zeus. "You must cut it open to let out the pain!"

Hephaestus pulled a blade from his belt, then hesitated. "Are you sure?"

"YES!" growled Zeus impatiently. "Hurry, I command you!"

Hephaestus nodded reluctantly.

SWISH went the blade, slicing neatly across Zeus' furrowed brow...

"Aaaah," sighed the king of the gods in relief – as

out of his head jumped a fierce young woman with dark hair and piercing eyes.

Hephaestus goggled.

She was dressed for battle and grasping a spear, ready for whatever the world might throw at her. Her quicksilver gaze took in her heavenly surroundings – then sparkled as she broke into a wide smile.

"Hello, Father. Hello, Brother," she said. "My name is Athena."

Zeus smiled back in delight, his headache already forgotten. "Athena, my daughter," he said warmly. "Welcome!"

Brave and clever, Athena soon made her mark among the other gods. She didn't flinch from a challenge, even if it came from one of the oldest, most powerful gods... gods like Poseidon, brother of Zeus, who ruled over seas and oceans.

Athena's tussle with Poseidon began when the peace of the gods' heavenly home was disturbed early one morning...

Bang-bang-bang... clatter-clang!

Unfamiliar sounds were drifting up from below. Curious, the gods peered down through the clouds to see what was going on.

Far below, on a hillside by the sea, the people of Greece were hard at work. Athena was intrigued. She loved observing humans and would sometimes go down to Earth and walk among them. Now, she looked on with interest as they scurried about, hammering, chiselling, marking things out. Huge blocks of stone were being cut into shape and hauled into position.

"What are they making?" wondered Zeus.

Athena's sharp eyes saw walls and columns rising up, doors being hung, roofs being tiled... "A city," she replied. "They're building a new city. It's going to be magnificent! Just look at those columns... and their tools are really ingenious. These people are *clever*. When they finish their city, I should become their patron."

Athena's eyes glazed over, dreamily. "They'll build me a magnificent temple. And when it's finished, they'll fill it with gifts and prayers of devotion. And in return, I'll watch over them and protect them. I'll teach them how to weave, and where to sail their ships, and how to build even greater buildings," Athena went on. "And if they have to go to war, I'll tell them the best strategies for dealing with their enemies..."

"Don't be ridiculous," came a snort from behind her. Athena turned and saw a powerful figure, dressed in a sea-green robe, with a long beard that frothed and curled like sea foam. It was Poseidon.

He too had been watching the building works. He had especially noted the huge temple being built in pride of place on top of the highest hill. It was a marvel of shining white stone, with colossal columns and elaborate carvings.

Poseidon thought greedily of that temple and the offerings that would fill it, and glared at Athena. "A great city should have a *great* patron. One of the first gods – not a mere newcomer. And they're building by the *sea* – so of course that patron should be *me*."

Athena gazed back at Poseidon, undaunted. The sea god was as mighty as the oceans he ruled, with a tempestuous temper. What he wanted, he usually got. But Athena knew she could outwit him. She just needed to make it a contest of brains, rather than brawn... and to ensure Poseidon didn't fly into a fit of rage over it.

"So, Uncle, we both have a claim to this city. How shall we decide between us?"

Poseidon raised the sharp, three-pronged trident

he carried and gave it a little shake.
"We could fight for it,"
he boomed.

Athena nodded. "We
could," she agreed calmly.
"It would be the traditional
solution. But you know,
this is really about the people
of the city," she went on.
"Perhaps we should appear
before them and let *them* decide?"

Poseidon considered the idea. He imagined
himself and Athena appearing side by side – his
huge muscular form towering above her. It appealed
to his vanity, as Athena had known it would. Surely
the people would choose him, mighty Poseidon,
the divine ruler of the seas and oceans, and not this
young upstart!

"Very well," he agreed.

But Athena hadn't finished. "To help the people
decide, I propose we each make the city a gift.

Then we can ask the people to say which gift they like best, and the giver of that gift shall become their patron."

Poseidon thought of the gifts he could bestow. He could give the people of the city endless fish to fill their bellies, or fair winds for their sailing ships... or, perhaps, he could even conjure up a new kind of animal for them, like the sea-horses that pulled his chariot below the waves. Athena was clever, but she did not have his powers.

He dipped his chin. "All right."

Athena nodded gravely. "Let us meet the people tomorrow to present our gifts."

Poseidon barely heard her. Looking down upon the dusty, sun-scorched ground around the city, he had just realized what his gift would be...

Water! People couldn't live without it. He was the god of the sea – he would give the city its own supply of water. "Ha!" he chuckled. "Athena will never better that."

Before deciding on her own gift, Athena went

down to the city to study the people. A dark-haired stranger, she wandered among the half-finished stone buildings and the little wooden huts of the workers, watching and listening. As dusk fell, they put down their tools, and began lighting fires and lamps. Voices chattered and delicious smells wafted from cooking pots.

Athena frowned thoughtfully. She could see these people needed many things. Food to eat; fuel to burn on fires and in lamps; wood to build their homes and boats...

"Perhaps I can give them *all* of that with the right gift," she mused.

After considering, she found the master builder in charge of the site, and explained how she and Poseidon were each going to give the city a gift...

"Whoever gives the best gift will become your city's new patron. We will appear on the hill by your new temple at daybreak."

"Thank you," said the builder, bowing low to the goddess. "It will be a great privilege." When he straightened up again, she was gone. "This will be interesting," he thought to himself, as he hurried off to spread the word.

Well before dawn, huge crowds gathered around the temple on the hill. As the sun broke over the horizon, the rivals appeared. Poseidon arrived in a rush of salty sea air. Athena stepped lightly out of nowhere in a shimmer of blue-white light. The crowd blinked and bowed respectfully.

Poseidon spoke first. "People of the city, behold my gift to you!" He raised his arm and hurled his trident towards a rocky crag.

CRRRRRACK! The rock sprang apart and a spring of cool, clear water bubbled up. It rushed over the dry ground, hissing around rocks and hurrying into gullies, creating a stream where

seconds ago there
had been only
dust and dirt and
trampled grass.
People blinked
in amazement.
"A spring!"
It was just what the city – built
among hot, dry hills – needed.
"Thank you!"
They ran over to touch the water
and make sure it was real. It felt cool
and wonderfully refreshing in the blazing
summer heat.
Eagerly, the master builder scooped
up a handful to taste. He put his
glistening hands to his mouth –
which twisted in shock.
"S-s-salt!" he stammered,
letting the rest splash onto
the ground.

The faces around him fell. A few others tried too, to make sure – but quickly spat the water out again. The builder was right. Poseidon, god of the sea, had given the city *sea* water.

The master builder turned to the god and bowed respectfully. It would not do to offend a god. "Thank you for your gift. It is a good gift. We may not be able to drink it, but it is always good to have water. We can use it for washing and cleaning."

"Now for my gift," said Athena. She raised her spear. The people nearest to her drew back cautiously – but she didn't throw it. Instead, she simply touched the tip to the ground before her.

Tap! Nothing happened.

Poseidon raised an eyebrow and chuckled. "At least my gift worked."

"Have patience," answered Athena coolly. "The best magic takes time."

Still nothing. Slowly, people began to turn away and chat.

"Looks as though Poseidon will be our patron,"

said one. There were murmurs of agreement.

"Look!" cried a little girl suddenly.

There, where the spear had touched the ground, the earth was trembling. A moment later, a tiny green shoot appeared. The onlookers gasped as it twisted upwards, thickening before their eyes into a gnarly-looking trunk. The trunk split into branches, and the branches into twigs. Then the twigs sprouted soft silvery-green leaves, that shimmered in the breeze. Here and there among the leaves hung clusters of little dark berries.

The master builder rubbed his eyes and stared. He had never seen a tree like it.

Now Athena spoke to the crowd. "People of the city, I give you the first olive tree. Its berries are tangy and delicious, to feed you. Crush them, and they will give you fragrant golden oil – to cook with, or to light your lamps. The wood is strong and good for carving. And its silver leaves will dance in the wind, to gladden your hearts."

"Thank you," said the master builder. "This is

Now Athena spoke to the crowd. "People of the city,
I give you the first olive tree."

a truly great gift." He looked around at his people, and they nodded. The answer was plain.

He cleared his throat, then spoke so all could hear. "Athena, we choose your gift. We would like you to be our patron – and we will name our city Athens after you."

Poseidon scowled and stormed away in a thunderous mood, muttering something about upstart girls and mountainous waves.

But if he did try to harm the city, Athena would defend it. She gave the people her most dazzling smile. With her help, she knew, these people would prosper. In time, Athens would become one of the greatest cities in the world. And you can still find groves of olive trees – and bubbling springs – there to this very day.

About the Stories

Gaia – the first of them all

The myth of Gaia comes from Hesiod, an Ancient Greek poet, who lived between 750 and 650 BCE. His poem, *The Theogony*, tells the story of the birth of the gods. In Ancient Greek art, Gaia is often shown rising from the earth or lying on the ground, surrounded by rich fruits.

Demeter and Persephone

This story is one of the oldest Greek myths and may date back as far as 1400 BCE. By about 700 BCE, the story was being sung as one of the *Homeric Hymns*, which were songs in praise of the gods. It went on to be retold in the first century CE by Ovid, a Roman poet, in his long poem, *The Metamorphoses*.

The Tasks of Psyche

The legend of Psyche comes from Latin author Apuleius, writing in the second century CE. His story went on to inspire many other writers and artists, including the Italian writer Boccaccio, who made it popular across Europe. In art, Psyche is often shown with the wings of a butterfly.

Daphne's Transformation

The earliest source of this myth is from Phylarchus, who lived in the 3rd century BCE. Later, the poet, Ovid, retold the legend in *The Metamorphoses*. In Ovid's version, Daphne prays to her father for help, but in the versions of Nonnus and Hyginus, two other Latin writers, she prays to Gaia for protection.

Circe the Sorceress

The sorceress, Circe, appears in many legends, including *The Odyssey*, a famous poem by the Ancient Greek poet, Homer. Composed around the 8th century BCE, the poem tells of Circe's encounter with Odysseus. Ovid's poem, *The Metamorphoses*, describes how Circe transforms Picus and Scylla. Her story's ending, as told here, comes from *The Telegony*, a long poem that followed on from *The Odyssey*.

Penelope's Tale

Penelope's story is mainly known from *The Odyssey*. There are other versions of her story, though, including those that appear in a book called *The Library of Greek Mythology* – a collection of Greek myths and legends compiled around the 2nd century CE. In some versions of Penelope's story, she is also said to be the mother of the god, Pan.

Artemis and the Hunt

A hymn by Callimachus tells the story of Artemis' childhood, while the tale of Artemis and the Aloadae comes from *The Library of Greek Mythology*.

Atalanta's Race

The story of Atalanta's race, and how she was turned into a lion, comes from Ovid's poem, *The Metamorphoses*. In a story in *The Library of Greek Mythology,* Atalanta also sailed with the hero Jason on a quest to find a fabled golden fleece.

Athena's Gift

Athena was the patron of several Greek cities, not just Athens, and appears in many myths. The story of her contest with Poseidon comes from *The Library of Greek Mythology*.

Brave and Brilliant Girls from the Greek Myths

Designed by Samantha Barrett
Cover illustration by Maria Surducan
Digital design: Nick Wakeford
Managing editor: Lesley Sims
Managing designer: Russell Punter